A Journey to Tooth Fairyland : Believe

By
L Rae Thompson

Dedication

To my niece Cortney
who reawakened me to childlike wonder.

Thanks Suzanne
for helping to make this book more magical.

And,
thanks Roger for pushing me to reach my goal.

Illustrator : Bamanimax

Cortney jumped off of the school bus wearing her mahogany grin as her braids flapped in the wind.
She ran into the house screaming,
"Aunt Sissy, my tooth is loose."

She opened her mouth, reached inside and wiggled one of her top front teeth.

"Does it hurt?" asked Aunt Sissy.

"No. Not one bit", she replied.

"Okay just leave it alone and we will keep an eye on it."

Later that night Cortney brushed her teeth with extra gentleness around the wiggly tooth. She asked, "Aunt Sissy, my friend Sarah says my tooth is going to fall out. But I don't want to lose my tooth!"

"Don't worry Cortney! Whenever you lose a tooth a new, bigger, stronger tooth takes the place of the tooth that fell out. This will be your Forever Tooth. You must always take special care of it." Aunt Sissy leaned over to kiss her on the forehead. Cortney felt Aunt Sissy's kiss and noticed her necklace, with a tooth charm dangling.

Cortney gazed at the baby silver tooth as it swung gently in front of her eyes. Aunt Sissy hugged Cortney close to her and said, "Change is a part of life, and so is loss", "Now it is time for bedtime. Tomorrow we go to the park!"

Cortney knelt by her bed to say her prayers before going to sleep. "Dear God let me keep my tooth. Amen." She climbed under the covers and fell fast asleep.

The next morning, the sun beamed into Cortney's window, she sat up in her bed and sang, "It's Saturday. It's Saturday." She ran to her Aunt Sissy's bedroom and shouted, "Aunt Sissy, I am ready to go to the park."

Aunt Sissy smiled and stretched. "Then I'd better get up and make us some scrumptious chocolate chip pancakes, before we go." And after they ate lots and lots of pancakes they walked to the park hand in hand.

At the park, Cortney skipped to the swings. "Push me Aunt Sissy. I want to swing high up into the sky."

Cortney ran to hang from the Monkey bars next. But, on the third rung her hand slipped. She felt herself falling but Aunt Sissy was right below to catch her.
"That was a close one, Aunt Sissy!"

She reached around Aunt Sissy's neck to give her a hug. Aunt Sissy's necklace got tangled in her hand. The chain broke and the necklace fell to the ground. Cortney knelt and picked it up off of the ground. She took a closer look. The shiny, silver charm in the shape of a tooth had letters on it. "What does it say, Aunt Sissy?"
Cortney grabbed it."

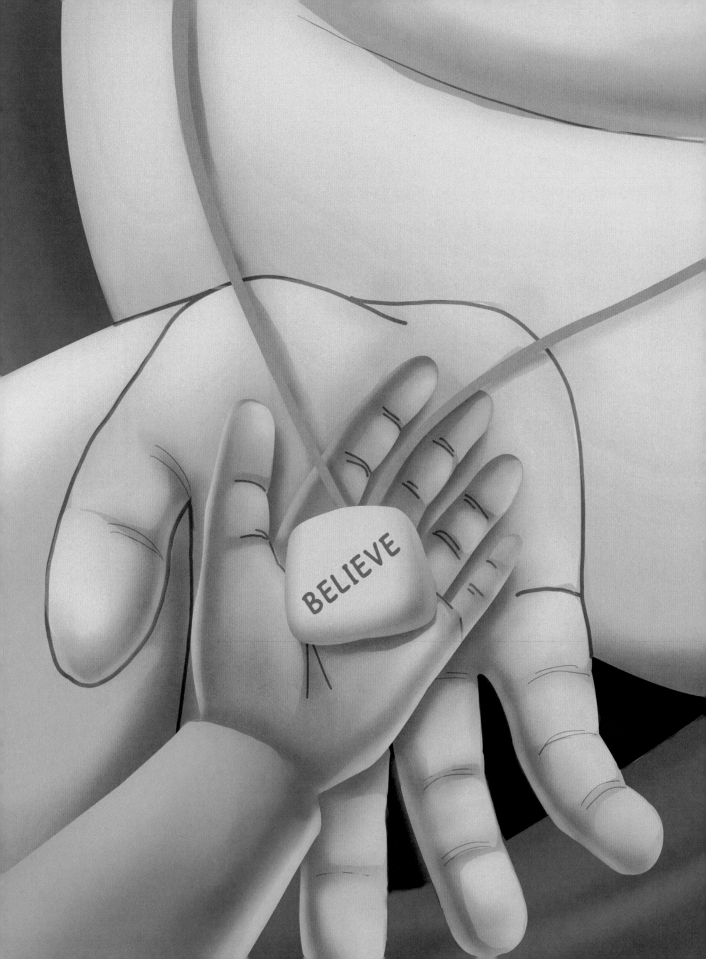

"The letters spell Believe", said Aunt Sissy.

"Where did you get this necklace, Auntie?"

"I think it was given to me from my mom or my aunt when I was your age. I can't remember. You see, I once lost my first tooth, too."

"Did your mouth hurt when your tooth fell out?"

"No, not one bit. It was loose like yours and one morning it fell out. Then a new, bigger, stronger, grown-up tooth took its place, my Forever Tooth. Look, it's right here. I still have it." Cortney looked as Aunt Sissy pointed to her Forever Tooth.

After a fun day playing at the park, Cortney and Aunt Sissy sat down for dinner. Cortney's favorite meal was on the table -chicken nuggets, corn and broccoli. Just as she was chewing the last stalk of broccoli Cortney felt something hard. Very, very hard. CRUNCH, CRUNCH!

"Oh no. My tooth! My tooth fell out Aunt Sissy!" And suddenly there it was. Cortney's small tooth laying in her small palm.

"Oh this is an exciting day! This is what we have been waiting for!" Aunt Sissy reached into the kitchen drawer and handed Cortney a small, purple bag that had letters printed on it. "What does it say, Aunt Sissy?"

"It says 'Cortney's Tooth'. Now put the tooth into the bag and hide it under your pillow tonight."

"Why?" asked Cortney.

"Oh that is a surprise. You must wait to find out."

Cortney brushed her teeth and said her prayers early that night. She very gently placed the purple bag with the tooth inside under her pillow and closed her eyes tightly. She checked three more times to see if her tooth was in a good place under her pillow and finally closed her eyes for sleep.

SWOOSH, SWOOSH, SWOOSH. Cortney heard this sound in the dark room and opened her eyes. Her eyes became as large as saucers. "W-who are you?"

There stood this tiny, beautiful, brown fairy with braids, a star-tipped wand, and glittering wings that fluttered gently on her back. In a musical, quiet voice she said, "I'm Jacquetta". "I'm here to pick up your tooth."

"Why?"

"Why, it's my job."

"Please don't take my tooth", cried Cortney. And small tears popped onto her cheeks.
With raised eyebrows the tooth fairy kindly said, "Don't cry. Instead, why don't you come with me?"

Jacquetta waved her star-tipped wand and sprinkled glitter fairy dust onto Cortney. She became as tiny as Jacquetta.

Jacquetta took Cortney's hand. SWOOSH, SWOOSH, Zooooom! Cortney and Jacquetta drifted silently out of the window and up into the velvet dark, starry sky. Whoosh. They looked like shooting stars.

"Jacquetta, where are we going?" asked Cortney.

"We are going to Fairyland."

The darkened sky began to lighten into a cloudless blue sky. Fluttering sounds echoed all around them. Then, Cortney saw hundreds of tooth fairies flying around them, like a dance of butterflies. A few called out, "Hi Jacquetta. Welcome home."

Jacquetta and Cortney landed softly in front of a red and yellow mushroom cap. They began to walk down a springy, grassy road. A purple river flowed beside the road with tiny green fish splashing in the water.

She heard a low, tup-tup-psss-psss. The sound became louder the further they walked.

Just over the hill and all at once, Cortney saw huge brown barrels filled with tiny teeth surrounding plowed fields. Each barrel had a word printed on it - diente, dent, 牙, س, jino, zahn,....

Pointing Cortney asked, "What do the letters on the barrels say?"

"Well, each barrel is printed with the word 'TOOTH' in a different language," answered her tooth fairy. One barrel for each language in the world," answered Jacquetta.

Her eyes grew rounded as she said, "Wow!"

Garden fairies flitted everywhere between the rows of fields while filling their backpacks. As they wandered the rows, the fairies pulled on strings attached to their backpacks. Tup-tup-tup-tup-tup sounded as they dropped a tooth into the soil. Psss-psss-pssss sounded as a beam of light flashed glittery fairy dust sprinkled onto the tooth.

"What are they doing?"

"They are planting children's teeth picked up by the tooth fairies, from all around the world."

"But why," asked Cortney.

If you look over there, you will see." Jacquetta said pointing. Cortney looked over to another field. Out popped hundreds of buds! The buds unfolded into flowers, in every color from the rainbow and even some colors she had never seen before. In the centers were sparkling, mini tooth fairies with flickering lights. Hoooo, hoooo, hooo...they were all flying off towards a palace over the hill.

"Can we go with them?" Cortney asked.

"Not right now," said her tooth fairy.

As they continued walking, Cortney and Jacquetta came upon a lovely dark brown fairy dressed in deep purple with gold wings. He smiled and said, "Hello Jacquetta."

Jacquetta responded, "Hello Jesse."

"Who is your friend?" asked Jesse.

"I'm Cortney. Pleased to meet you." said Cortney with a smile.

"It's a pleasure to meet you Cortney." Jesse asked, "What brings you to Fairyland?"

"Tooth Fairy Jacquetta brought me because I was not ready to let go of my tooth", explained Cortney.

"So tell me, why do you want to keep your tooth?"

Cortney answered, "I need it just in case my new tooth does not grow in", answered Cortney.
"And besides, it is mine."

"Ho, ho, ho", chuckled Jesse. "I once had a child, a very long time ago, who did not want to let go of her tooth either. I believe her name was Sissy," said Jesse.

"Cortney every tooth gives birth to a new fairy. And every fairy adds magic to the world. The world is more beautiful when filled with magic, don't you think?" asked Jacquetta.

"Along with adding more magic to the world you will get a bigger, stronger, grown-up tooth to take the place of your tiny tooth. This will be your Forever Tooth. Isn't that magical?" Jesse added while twirling.

"But-but what if my tooth does not grow back."
Jacquetta reached into a hidden pocket in her wings. She
handed Cortney a gold coin and said, "This is my promise
that your Forever Tooth will grow."

Jesse reached around to his golden wings and put his
hand into a hidden pocket. He pulled out a silver necklace
with a silver charm shaped like a tooth hanging from it.
Jesse handed Cortney the necklace and closed her
fingers around it tightly.

"This looks exactly like the necklace my Aunt Sissy has",
exclaimed Cortney. "And these letters look like the same
letters on her charm! I know what it says. It says,
BELIEVE."

Jacquetta and Jesse smiled, fluttered their wings and
said, "YES, we know."

Cortney turned to her tooth fairy and asked,
"May I plant my tooth?"

"Yes."

Jacquetta, Jesse and Cortney returned to the field.
Cortney kissed her tiny tooth goodbye and dropped it
into the soil - tup. Jacquetta flashed the tooth with her
light and glittery fairy dust burst from the star-tipped
wand. PSSS! She recited, "Zinga-de-zing. Pinga-de-ping.
Tinga-de-ting. Tiny tooth TRANSFORM!"

"Thank you Cortney. You just added a little more magic to the world. Now it's time to take you back home."

"Can I come back again?" asked Cortney.

"If you are not sure about your next tooth,
I will bring you back."

"Yes. I would love that."

Jesse hugged Cortney goodbye and suddenly, Jacquetta and she took flight again. Faster than light, they were back in her bedroom. Jacquetta waved her star-tipped wand and with light and glittery fairy dust Cortney returned to regular size. Jacquetta tucked the covers snugly around Cortney and wished her sweet dreams. And then Jacquetta was gone!

Cortney, of course, fell into a very deep sleep.

The sun crept lazily into Cortney's room the next morning. Cortney sat upright in her bed and immediately reached under her pillow. There she found a gold coin nestled in her purple tooth fairy bag.

She ran into Aunt Sissy's bedroom. Her eyes were shining as bright as the sun, as she said "Guess what Aunt Sissy, I saw the Tooth Fairy last night."

Aunt Sissy said,"You did?"

Cortney held out her hand with the gold coin in her palm and said, "Yes. A tiny, beautiful, brown fairy with braided hair, a star-tipped wand, and glittering wings that fluttered gently on her back gave me this gold coin. She said it was a promise that my Forever Tooth would grow in."

Cortney reached up to give her aunt a kiss. Aunt Sissy looked down and said, "What is that around your neck?"

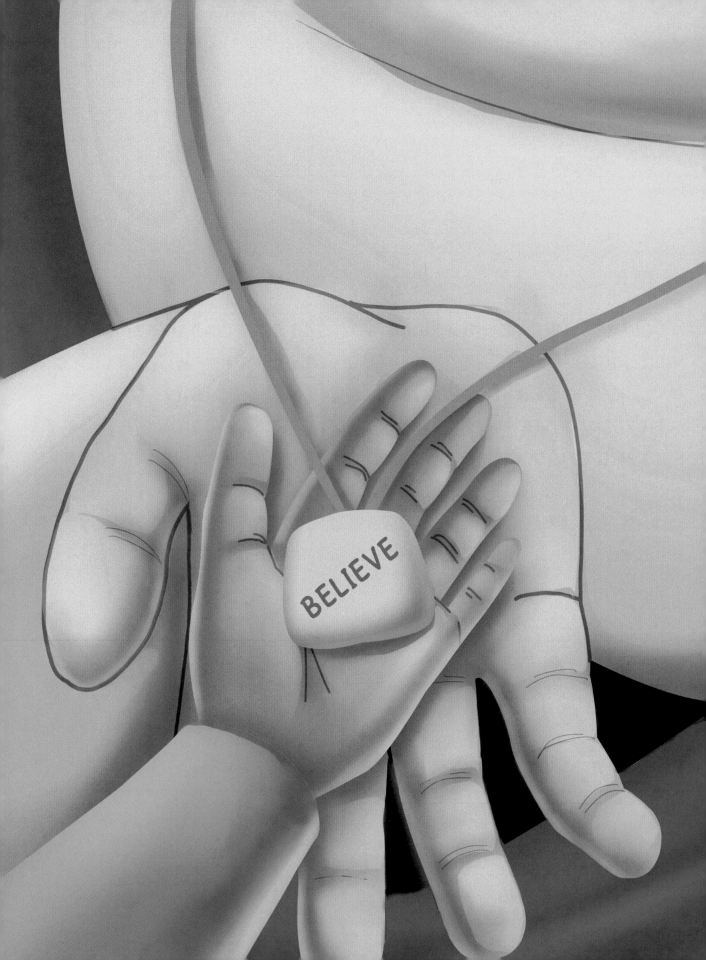

Cortney touched the silver necklace with the tooth charm. Jesse, a beautiful, brown fairy dressed in deep purple with sparkling wings, gave me this necklace. "It looks just like yours, Aunt Sissy! And, it has the same letters as yours does on the tooth charm."

Aunt Sissy looked at her, with surprise on her face. They read the word written on the charm together: BELIEVE.

And, at that moment Aunt Sissy remembered the night she too took a trip to Fairyland with her tooth fairy Jesse.

Made in the USA
Middletown, DE
22 April 2022